Jack & The Beanstalk

Retold & Illustrated by John Patience

There was once a boy called Jack who lived with his widowed mother in a broken down little cottage. They were very poor. In fact, the only thing they had in the world was a cow which gave them milk. Alas, the day came when the cow's milk ran dry and Jack's mother decided that the best thing to do was to sell her. So Jack set out to market with firm instructions to ask a good price for the cow. He hadn't gone more than a mile or two down the main road when he met with an odd little man. "That's a fine looking animal you have there," he exclaimed. "Yes, indeed she is," replied Jack. "I'm taking her to market." "Give her to me," said the little man. "Take these five magic beans in exchange. Plant them and they will make your fortune." Before Jack could speak, the little man took the cow and disappeared.

Jack began to feel he had made a mistake. What would his mother say? He returned home with a heavy heart. "What? Back so soon!" exclaimed his mother. "How much did you get for the cow?" "Five magic beans," replied Jack. "You idiot! We needed money to buy food," cried Jack's mother. "How could you be so stupid?" She snatched the beans and tossed them out of the window and poor Jack was sent to bed without any supper. The next morning when Jack woke up his room looked strange. It was bathed in a sort of greenish light. Jack went to the window and what did he see? The most amazing thing — the beans had sprung up into an enormous beanstalk which reached up .. up .. up into the clouds. Taking care not to wake his mother, Jack dressed and clambered from his window ledge onto the beanstalk and began to climb it, for he was sure that the fortune the little man had promised him must be at the top of it.

Jack climbed higher and higher, not daring to look down in case he became dizzy and fell. At last he reached the other side of the clouds and saw a long road. He walked along it until he came to a huge castle. Jack walked up and knocked on the door. It was opened by an enormous woman. "Be off with you," she said. "My husband is a giant and he will gobble you up if he catches you." "Oh, please be kind. I am hungry. Give me something to eat," begged Jack. Well, the giant's wife took pity on Jack. She led him into the kitchen and gave him some bread and cheese. He had just finished eating when he heard the sound of footsteps coming along the passage, and a voice like thunder boomed out,

"Fee, fie, foe, fum.
I smell the blood of an Englishman.
Be he alive or be he dead,
I'll grind his bones to make my bread!"

"Goodness! It's my husband," cried the giant's wife. "Quick, hide in the oven."

The giant's wife calmed her husband, telling him that he was mistaken. "It must be your porridge that you can smell," she said, putting a bowl on the table for him. The giant grunted and sat down. When he had finished eating he took some bags from a cupboard and poured out a shower of gold coins from one of them. He began to count them. "One, two, three. ." As he did this he grew sleepy and, by the time he had reached ten, he was fast asleep and snoring loudly. Jack had been watching the giant through a crack in the oven door. Now he leaped on to the table and, snatching a bag of gold coins, he made off with it.

Jack and his mother lived off the gold for a long time, but at last it was all spent, and Jack decided that he must climb the beanstalk again. The giant's wife recognized Jack immediately and wanted to know what had happened to the bag of gold. "I'll tell you," said Jack, "if you give me breakfast." So the giant's wife took him in and fed him. And again there came the thudding of footsteps along the passage and Jack was forced to hide himself. After breakfast the giant's wife brought her husband a pet hen. "Lay, little hen," commanded the giant and the hen laid an egg of pure, glittering gold. After a while the giant fell asleep. Then Jack crept out from his hiding place, caught hold of the wonderful hen, ran from the castle, slid down the beanstalk and was safe and sound in his mother's garden.

Jack's mother was delighted with the hen which lay golden eggs. "We will never be poor again," she said. But before long Jack grew restless again and determined to climb the beanstalk. He realized that the giant's wife would not be pleased to see him, so he waited until she came out to hang out her washing, then crept into the castle and hid himself in a copper cauldron. Soon the giant came home and, sniffing the air, he bellowed,

"Fee, fie, foe, fum
I smell the blood of an Englishman."

But his wife assured him that he was mistaken. So he sat down to his breakfast, ate it and then called out. "Wife, bring me my harp." She brought it and placed it on the table. "Sing, harp," commanded the giant and the harp sang sweetly, lulling the giant off to sleep.

Then Jack crept quietly out of the cauldron and tip-toeing over to the table, he snatched the harp and ran off with it. But this time he got a surprise, for the harp called out loudly, "Master, master!" and the giant woke up. Fear made Jack run like the wind, but the giant came lumbering after him, roaring for his blood. Jack leaped onto the beanstalk and started to climb down. The beanstalk began to shake and

creak and sway around as if it was caught in a hurricane — the giant was climbing down after him! Faster and faster went Jack. "Mother," he called, leaping to the ground. "Bring me the axe."

Taking the axe, Jack swung it at the beanstalk and in three strokes he brought it toppling down from the sky. With a terrible roar, the giant came down too. The ground shook and the giant made a hole so deep that he never got out of it. The beanstalk never grew again, but it didn't matter very much, because the harp sang beautifully and the hen continued to lay golden eggs, so that Jack and his mother were never poor again.